Shabbat

WRITTEN AND ILLUSTRATED BY

Miriam Nerlove

Albert Whitman & Company

Morton Grove, Illinois

For Hannah and Eleanor, with love.

My thanks to many, especially Sandy Kanter of Rosenblum's World of Judaica, Chicago, and Irene Sufrin, Director of the Learning Center of Solomon Schechter Day School, Skokie, Illinois.

Library of Congress Cataloging-in-Publication Data
Nerlove, Miriam.
Shabbat / written and illustrated by Miriam Nerlove.
p. cm.
ISBN 0-8075-7324-8
1. Sabbath—Juvenile Literature. I. Title.
BM685.N38 1998   296.4'1—dc21   98-14412
CIP

The illustrations were done in watercolors.
The design is by Scott Piehl.

Albert Whitman & Company is also the publisher of The Boxcar Children® Mysteries.
For more information about all our fine books, visit us at www.awhitmanco.com.

I love Shabbat! It comes each week—
a time to rest and play.
We like to be together on
Shabbat, my favorite day!

Shabbat started long ago,
when God created the world...

For six days God worked hard to make the sun and moon, the trees,

animals and people, too,
soft clouds and stars and seas.

On the seventh day, God rested—
and so do we.

On Friday we prepare for Shabbat...

We clean the house; I help Mom dust.
We try to make things neat.
I even give our dog a bath,
so she'll smell nice and sweet!

I get to knead the challah dough;
Mom puts the chicken in to roast.
We make a noodle kugel, too—
the dish my brother likes the most!

It's time to wash up
and get dressed.
My grandparents come:
"Good Shabbos, dear!"

The sun is setting
pink and red;
it's getting late.
Shabbat is near.

I hear a key turn in the lock;
I know it's Daddy coming home.

The door swings open, and I see
that Daddy's here! "Shabbat Shalom!"

We gather in the dining room;
Mom puts a lace scarf on her head.
She lights two candles just before
this Sabbath blessing's said:

Praised are you, Adonai our God, Ruler of the universe,
who has sanctified our lives through your commandments,
commanding us to kindle the Sabbath lights.

It's time to say the Kiddush now,
and Daddy holds the silver cup.
He says this blessing over wine,
before I drink my grape juice up!

*Praised are you, Adonai our God, Ruler of
the universe, who creates the fruit of the vine.*

Hamotzi is the prayer we say
before we eat the bread.
The challah is uncovered,
and this prayer of thanks is said:

Praised are you, Adonai our God, Ruler of the
universe, who brings forth bread from the earth.

Then we eat our Sabbath meal; we talk and laugh a lot.
It's good to be together for this special time, Shabbat!

I wake up early Saturday;
I'll wear my nicest dress.
We go to synagogue today;
I like to look my best.

At synagogue we greet our friends.
I wave and say, "Hello!"
"Good Shabbos!" or "Shabbat Shalom!"
to everyone I know.

The cantor sings, the rabbi reads—
I love to hear him speak.
I know a lot of prayers by heart
because we come each week.

The cantor holds the Torah high
for everyone to see.
We follow him around the room;
my parents smile at me.

The service ends and we go home
for a peaceful afternoon.

We'll rest and play until we see
three stars beside the moon.

Havdalah marks the Sabbath's end,
and this is what we do:
we light a braided candle and
we smell sweet spices, too.

An overflowing cup of wine
is sweet and helps us bless
a brand new week—may it be filled
with peace and happiness.

Shavuah tov—a good week,
until our next Shabbat!

About Shabbat

The Jewish Sabbath begins at sundown every Friday. Known as *Shabbat* (shah-BAHT) in Hebrew and *Shabbos* (SHAH-biss) in Yiddish, the word means "rest."

Shabbat is one of the earliest of Jewish traditions. Jews believe that God created the world in six days and rested on the seventh. By doing the same themselves, the Jewish people believe they are honoring God.

The Shabbat candles are a reminder of the creation of light at the beginning of the world, and their lighting on Friday evening signifies the beginning of Shabbat. The *Kiddush* (kee-DOOSH or KID-dush) blessing over wine is a reminder of the holiness of Shabbat. Kiddush means "holy" in Hebrew. The wine's sweetness is a reminder of the sweetness of life.

On Shabbat a blessing called *Hamotzi* (hah-MOH-tsi), which means "the bringing forth," is said over two loaves of bread, each called a *challah* (KHAH-lah). Challah means "dough" in Hebrew. Pieces of bread are torn off and passed around so that everyone may share in this food, representing the abundance God provides.

On Shabbat, people go to the synagogue to pray. Shabbat ends when three stars appear in the sky on Saturday evening. *Havdalah* (hav-DAH-lah), which means "division" or "separation" in Hebrew, is the prayer that marks the end of Shabbat and the beginning of a new work week.

Just as God began Creation with light, and Shabbat is begun with lighting candles, so Jews begin a new week by lighting a long braided candle specially made for Havdalah. Wine is blessed as a reminder of the sweet holiness of Shabbat. The overflowing Kiddush cup symbolizes a wish for a week of plenty. A small wooden or silver box filled with sweet-smelling spices is passed around to replenish a spirit that is diminished by the departure of Shabbat.

Havdalah is a wonderful way to bring the family together at the end of Shabbat, to share in some last peaceful moments before the start of a busy new week.